ZOEY THE MONSTER MASHER

Written and Illustrated

By

Katrina Carter

Copyright © 2019

In a town crawling with MONsTers

There lived a Hero brave enough to take them on

One by One.

I'm ZOey.

I have cOOl goggles,
awesome bOOts
and
Major MONsTer
maShing Moves.

You see some time ago

MONsTers (ooey, icky, gooey MONsTers)

attacked my town.

And I knew I had to save it.

I was so good at maShing MONsTers

that I could even maSh them in my sleep!

But when I was awake MONsTers didn't stand a chance.

Like the time I did some awesome maShing on

The super slippery flubber MONsTer

in Mrs. Marshall's backyard.

Or the time I saved the school from

The Giant
Pink Four
Eyed
BlOb
MONsTer!

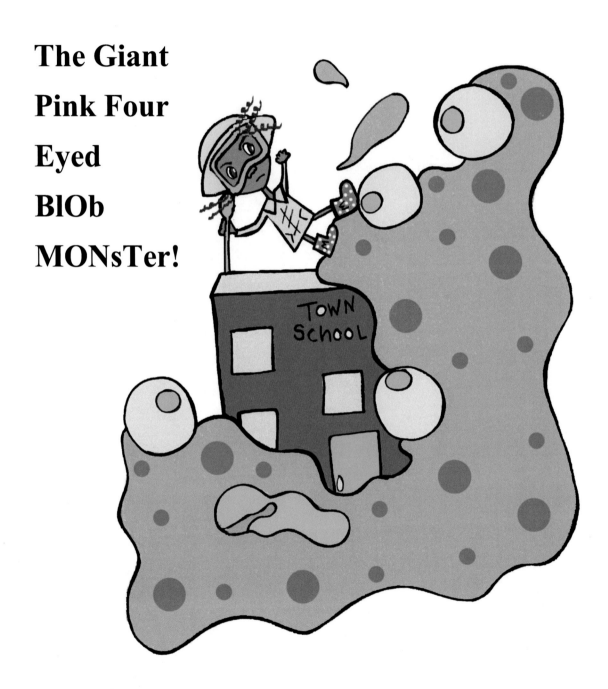

Oh and let's not forget that one time I did some

serious maShing on

The

sTinky sTink seaweed

MONsTer Twins!!

That was a hard job, they were really stinky.

I maShed every MONsTer

one by one.

with the help of my

gOOp guard safety gear

an aleRt meter

to let me know when MONsTers were close by.

and most importantly the MOST important

of ALL things for

maShing MONsTers

One pair of

gOOp guShing, squiSh squaShing,

Major maShtastic bOOts!

Even the ooiest, gooiest, slipperiest MONsTers

didn't stand a chance with them!

And so just like that

my town was safe and happy again.

Until one day…

MONsTers

Were

Everywhere !!

There were **Big Ones**

small Ones

Sticky Ones   **Slimy Ones**

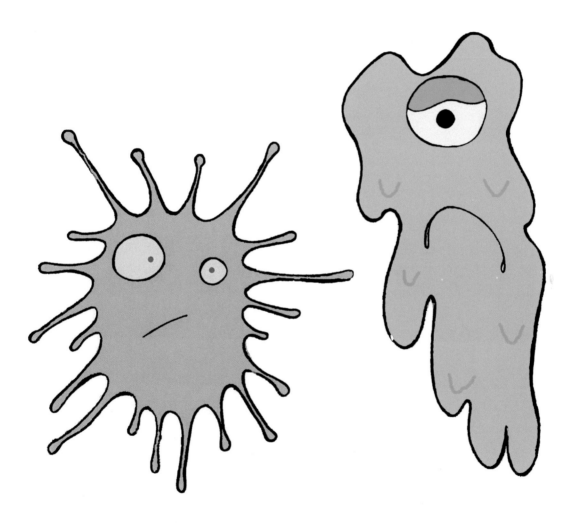

Lumpy Ones   **Bumpy Ones**

The aleRt meter was going haywire!

OH NO!

What was I to do?!

I'd never had to fight
so many MONsTers at one time
before.

But I had no choice, I had to
save my town!

It was time to **gear UP.**

gOOp guard
safety hat
check √

gOOp guard
safety goggles
check √

gOOp guard
safety jacket
check √

gOOp guShing

squiSh squaShing

Major maShtastic bOOts

Double check √√

But there were so many MONsTers, even with all

of my gear I was going to need **backup.**

It was time to bring out my Top Secret

smaSh MONsTers

to **smitheReens**

In case of

MONsTer Emergency **Only**

Super squiSher
5000!

and nothing got past that!

With my Moves, bOOts and Super squiSher

I was ready.

Armed with Courage and Bravery

I followed the aleRt meter to where all

of the MONsTers had gathered and I…

baShed them!

squiShed them!

squaShed them!

cruShed them!

craShed them!

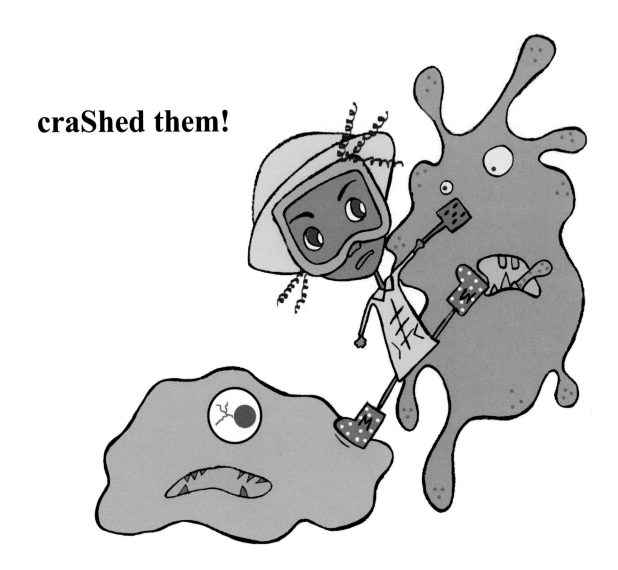

smuShed them!

smaShed them!

And

maShed them!!

Those mangy MONsTers didn't know what hit them!

And by the time I was done I was covered in

gOOp, gOOk, eyeballs, glop, and slop.

But I didn't mind as long as my town and the people I loved were safe.

And they always would be.

Because even after kicking some Major MONsTer butt I had a
sneaky feeling more MONsTers would show up soon enough

and I'd be ready.

Made in the USA
Middletown, DE
28 October 2020

22918985R00020